WILLIAM KOTZWINKLE in the past few years has been recognized as one of our most important writers. He is the author of ELEPHANT BANGS TRAIN. HERMES 3000. NIGHTBOOK, THE FAN MAN. SWIMMER IN THE SECRET SEA. DR. RAT. FATA MORGANA, HERR NIGHTINGALE AND THE SATIN WOMAN. JACK IN THE BOX. and a novel based on the screenplay for E.T.: THE EXTRATERRESTRIAL. as well as the juvenile stories THE FIREMEN. THE SHIP THAT CAME DOWN THE GUTTER. ELEPHANT BOY, THE DAY THE GANG GOT RICH, THE OLDEST MAN AND OTHER TIMELESS STORIES, THE RETURN OF CRAZY HORSE, UP THE ALLEY WITH JACK AND JOE, THE NAP MASTER. THE ANTS WHO TOOK AWAY TIME. DREAM OF DARK HARBOR and THE SUPREME. SUPERB, EXALTED AND DELIGHTFUL. ONE AND ONLY MAGIC BUILDING.

Other Avon and Bard Books by
William Kotzwinkle

ELEPHANT BANGS TRAIN
THE FAN MAN
NIGHT BOOK
SWIMMER IN THE SECRET SEA

THE LEOPARD'S TOOTH

WILLIAM KOTZWINKLE

 A BARD BOOK/PUBLISHED BY AVON BOOKS

AVON BOOKS
A division of
The Hearst Corporation
959 Eighth Avenue
New York, New York 10019

Text Copyright © 1976 by William Kotzwinkle
Illustrations Copyright © 1976 by Joe Servello
Designed by Victoria Gomez
Published by arrangement with Clarion Books
Library of Congress Catalog Card Number: 75-25504
ISBN: 0-380-01910-8

First Camelot Printing, March, 1978
First Bard Printing, February, 1983

BARD TRADEMARK REG. U. S. PAT. OFF. AND IN
OTHER COUNTRIES, MARCA REGISTRADA, HECHO EN
U. S. A.

Printed in the U. S. A.

OP   10 9 8 7 6 5 4 3 2 1

The Leopard's Tooth

New York City, 1911

W ell, Charles, is your gear all packed?" Doctor Pickett stood at the window of their house on Riverside Drive, gazing down at the street below. A horse-drawn carriage was slowly winding its way along the pavement.

"Yes, sir," said Charles. Hearing the clip-clop of the horse's hooves, he joined his father at the window. Together they watched the carriage approaching, and Charles's heart began to beat faster. He was certainly ready and had been for several days. He'd packed, unpacked, and packed again, arranging and rearranging his tropical jacket and pants, his bush helmet, his compass, and ax.

The carriage came alongside their house. The driver

was hunched at the reins, his top hat tipped down over his eyes. However, the carriage didn't stop but continued past the Pickett house and on up the Drive.

Doctor Pickett pulled out his gold pocket watch. "Sir Henry is late. He must have had trouble getting a carriage."

But Charles knew that Sir Henry would not fail to come, even if that great English gentleman had to carry his luggage on his back. Sir Henry Turnbull was one of the foremost authorities in the world on old bones—long-buried bones of men who'd lived lost ages ago. Charles and Doctor Pickett were to accompany him on his forthcoming expedition to Africa. Today was sailing day. Sir Henry would certainly show up. He was not a man to let anything stand in his way.

The door to the front room opened, and Mr. Wyman, the butler, entered quietly. He was a rough-looking man, with a long scar over his eyebrow and a flattened-out nose. He'd been a prizefighter and a sailor and a tramp, and the Picketts had met him in Riverside Park one day where Wyman had been engaged in placing a fallen bird's nest into a tree. Doctor Pickett, believing that a man who was kind to animals could be trusted, offered Wyman the position of butler, cook, and bottlewasher in the Pickett house. Wyman, who'd been down on his luck and coming through his boots, had happily accepted the position.

"Will you gentlemen have some tea?" he asked, giving Charles a sly wink. He knew the boy's spirit was straining at the bit, eager to be off to the high seas.

"Thanks, Wyman," said Doctor Pickett. He took the offered tea over to the window where he resumed his post, one foot on the window ledge, eyes turned toward the street below.

"There's a postcard for you from Mrs. Pickett," said Wyman, presenting the card to Charles on a small silver tray.

Charles picked it up and looked first at the photograph of some old stones and rubble surrounded by sand. Then he turned the postcard over and read his mother's neatly written note:

> Dear Charles,
>
> This is King Khasekhemui's temple. All that's left of it is a granite doorpost. Nearby we found a line chiseled in a stone. ". . .and the youth became like a leopard." Odd the things one digs up. Your trip starts soon, doesn't it? Give my best to Sir Henry.
>
> Affectionately,
> Helen

Charles laid the postcard down with a smile. His mother was an archeologist and had made trips to the temples of Egypt, South America, and Mexico. School work had always kept Charles from going on these trips, and whenever his mother returned, he would spend the rest of the year dreaming over the ancient bits of treasure she brought back with her. But this year he was off on his own, and Sir Henry Turnbull had promised they'd be finding bones that were 500,000 years old!

"How about a bite to eat?" asked Wyman, pouring tea for Charles.

"I'm too nervous to eat, Mr. Wyman."

"Your nerves will smooth out once you're sailing on the water. It's a good time of year for the trip. I've stood watch on board ship when the waves were as high as this house. You'd ride up on that wave, up, up, and up . . ." Wyman sent his hand up slowly through the air, then brought it down. ". . . and you'd come down—thump, thump, thump—and you'd be sure the ship was coming apart at the seams. Many a time I said to myself, this is it. We'll never get out of this one. And we always got out, matey." He touched Charles gently on the shoulder. "We always got out of her."

Wyman had told Charles many hair-raising tales of his adventures in foreign lands. And occasionally Wyman would entertain old shipmates in the little room he occupied in the rear of the Pickett home. These visitors were always strange, hard-boiled men who told fantastic stories, spinning them out to each other and to Charles who joined them in the back room as often as they invited him.

They were a motley crew, and Doctor Pickett's patients were often alarmed at seeing a small sinister man with an eye-patch entering the side door of the Pickett house; or were frightened by a swarthy old rascal with a gold ring in his ear and the tattoo of an eagle directly in the center of his bald head. But

Doctor Pickett assured his patients that everything was all right, that these men were "friends of the family."

The truth was Doctor Pickett was himself a lover of high adventure, though his medical practice did not allow him much time for traveling. So he welcomed the raggle-taggle bunch of vagabonds who visited Wyman, and he greatly enjoyed their wild stories of distant lands.

Something of the sailor's wanderlust must have rubbed off on the Doctor, for when Sir Henry Turnbull proposed an African trip, Doctor Pickett said yes. He'd known Sir Henry for years, from the day they'd met in the Museum of Natural History, before a display of ancient skulls. Whenever Sir Henry came to America he called on Doctor Pickett and always tried to coax him on a trip. This year he'd succeeded. Doctor Pickett arranged for another doctor to take his patients, and now he was waiting and ready. His wife would not be the only one to bring back lost treasures!

A sudden sound of gunshots filled the air. Wyman and Charles both jumped to the window beside Doctor Pickett. An automobile was coming up the drive!

It was a strange-looking iron box on wheels, explosions bursting out the rear of it and the driver sitting up near the engine, tightly clutching the steering wheel. Through the window behind the driver, Charles could see Sir Henry's huge pith helmet and bushy beard.

The driver brought the automobile to the curbstone in front of the Pickett house, the motor idling down, but continuing to blast smoke and fire out the tail pipe.

"She's a regular gunboat, isn't she," said Wyman.

"All right now," said Doctor Pickett, "let's get these trunks down to the street."

Charles and his father grabbed hold of one, and Wyman grabbed the other, raising it up to his shoulder as if it were no more than a bag of groceries. They proceeded down the stairs to the front door, where Sir Henry was already waiting, holding it open. He was a gray-bearded giant of a man, with a voice like a foghorn and the handshake of a bear. "Doctor Pickett, did you sleep last night?"

"Not a wink."

"Nor I," said Sir Henry. "Wyman, how are you today?"

"Fine, Sir Henry, and you?"

"Couldn't find a carriage, so I was forced to hire this infernal machine." He thrust his cane out at the backfiring car, striking it soundly on the fender.

The driver lowered the door to a storage compartment in the rear of the taxi, and the Pickett trunks were placed inside. Sir Henry's trunk—old, bruised, and covered with travel stickers—had been roped to the roof of the auto. The driver stood on the running board and checked the ropes once again, then turned to Sir Henry. "We're ready, sir."

"Gentlemen," said Sir Henry, bowing toward the rumbling vehicle. Charles and Doctor Pickett climbed in. Charles sat by the open window and Wyman came around beside it.

"*Doctor Pickett, did you sleep last night?*"

"Take care of yourself, lad."

There was a sudden grinding of gears, a tremendous bang, and the taxi leapt forward. Charles leaned out the window, turning backward to wave to Wyman. The old sailor stood in the middle of the Drive and tossed a sharp salute to Charles.

Doctor Pickett, waving from the other window, noticed a limping little man turning the corner onto the Drive. "There's old Captain Nugent," said the Doctor. "Coming to play cards with Wyman, I imagine." The doctor turned to his son. "Perhaps, Charles, we'll have a tale or two of our own to spin for them when we return."

The automobile made its way to the waterfront, terrifying horses right and left and drawing the abuse of numerous carriagemen. "There is our ship," said Sir Henry, as the auto turned toward a long wooden pier, beside which the S.S. *Elizabeth* was docked, her flags waving in the river wind. In a few moments Charles was standing on the pier, the shouts of the deckhands in his ears and the whole waterfront spectacle before his eyes. Great cartons of cargo were being swung into the ship's hold and smoke was starting to billow out of the stacks. He walked slowly up the gangplank with his father and Sir Henry. They were on their way to Africa at last!

1

The calm sea shimmered all around them, as if they were steaming along over an endless mirror. From his deck chair Charles could see tiny birds in the distance, skimming the water. The sight of them was punctuated by Sir Henry Turnbull's huge frame moving back and forth nervously along the ship's railing. Doctor Pickett, seated beside Charles, called out to the leader of the expedition, "You look like a caged animal, Sir Henry."

"Yes, and I feel like one too. But once you set foot on África's soil"—he gestured across the glistening mirror toward its outermost edge—"once you go deep into its forests, you'll be drawn to them again and again, as I am; drawn as if by a magician's spell."

Charles looked toward Sir Henry, expecting to see the jovial man's smiling gaze. But instead he saw a darkly troubled look in Sir Henry's eyes. It was only a passing cloud, however, blown away by the gentle sea wind.

Charles saw the troubled look return when their ship was within a day of the African shore. They were waiting for dessert in the ship's dining room. Doctor Pickett had removed a small slender book from his jacket and was glancing idly through it. "Interesting reading," he said, looking up at Charles and Sir Henry. "A British army doctor's experiences in Africa. I thought I'd better get an idea of what to expect." Doctor Pickett's gaze returned to the printed page of the little book until he found something that made him smile, and he raised his eyes again. "Do you know, Sir Henry, that magic is called the medicine of the jungle?"

Again it was only a momentary flicker in Sir Henry's eyes, but this time Charles saw it more distinctly, and he caught a note of apprehension in Sir Henry's voice, despite the smile on the scientist's face.

"I've had experience of jungle magic—or medicine, call it what you like," said Sir Henry. "It's a lot of silly nonsense. Here's our pie. I believe it's apple. Yes, most decidedly."

That evening the sea wind brought a strange smell to Charles as he stood at the ship's railing. For a moment, he thought that someone wearing strong perfume or cologne must have strolled the deck, but then he realized that the smell was everywhere. The ship seemed to have entered an invisible cloud of scent.

"That is Africa," said a soft voice behind him, and Sir Henry was suddenly at his side, having come up silently as a cat. They strained their eyes to make out some sign of land beyond them, but the horizon was a dark impenetrable curtain. Still the perfume continued to haunt the ship, even creeping through the portholes of Charles's cabin and following him into sleep.

When he stepped on deck the next morning, Charles saw the glistening jungle in the distance. As they came into port, the hot fragrant breath of the forest was overwhelming, and when his feet touched the ground, he was inside a steaming bouquet. Flowers hung everywhere with dewdrop diamonds sparkling upon them, and insects zoomed around their head as the expedition party found its way toward the hotel. They were at the mouth of the Congo River, at the sandy point called Banana. On the following day they would begin their trek into the heart of the lush, buzzing land.

That evening at dinner, they ate beside a garden filled with tame blue-faced monkeys, who were huddled around some leafy greens. The monkeys all had white mustaches across their upper lips and looked to Charles like little old men having a game of cards.

"We shall travel this route."

"We shall travel this route," said Sir Henry, running his finger along a map he'd spread on the table. Charles saw a winding blue line, which Sir Henry identified as the Congo River. "We follow the river—to here," said Sir Henry, pointing to a lake in the midst of the green jungle.

Just as Sir Henry's finger touched the map, a great cat roared in the nearby jungle. It was a chilling sound, and the monkeys scattered into the treetops when they heard it. But the roar did not come again. Quietly, the monkeys peeked out of the leaves. Sir Henry broke the spell with a hearty laugh. "Well, Doctor Pickett, a jungle magician would tell you that roar meant something."

Doctor Pickett smiled. "And what does it mean?"

"That the cat is hungry." Sir Henry toyed with his monocle. "But a witch doctor would tell you differently. He would say that at just this spot here" —Sir Henry again pointed with his finger to the jungle lake—"a cat awaits me."

Charles almost jumped out of his chair when the great cat roared again.

2

O n the following day, they moved upriver in the little steamboat, *Maria*. The jungle wall slipped slowly by, as they sat on the rear deck with a fourth man. "John Handy," he said, introducing himself, "of the Handy Circus."

Sir Henry smiled, tapping his cane lightly on the steamboat's rail. "And you have come here for . . .?"

"Elephants, lions, leopards." John Handy paused. He was a tall Englishman, with a nose like a hawk's beak and cold steel-blue eyes to match. "I'm the animal trainer," he said, with a gaze that was almost hypnotic, as if his willpower were gathered in his eyes, waiting for some animal to attack.

Charles looked toward the bright jungle shoreline,

where countless flowers of every color were opening in the morning sun. It was hard to believe that behind such a lovely veil there were deadly cats prowling.

"I hope you'll catch the leopard who's after me," said Sir Henry with his usual laugh, his whole stomach rumbling.

"Is there a particular one who dislikes you?" asked John Handy, smiling.

"It's not the leopard who dislikes me. It's the witch doctor of the Tambo tribe. We had a bit of a disagreement my last time out here. The old boy rattled some beads and said that I'd return to Africa again and again, until a leopard finally devoured me. What nonsense, eh?"

But John Handy did not smile. In fact, the animal trainer's cold eyes became suddenly fierce, as if he were staring at some invisible animal that had suddenly sprung onto the deck in front of him.

Several hundred miles up the great river, *Maria* pulled into shore at a spot called One Thousand Huts, a village that was close to the lake Sir Henry was seeking. The steamer was docked for much of the afternoon, during which Sir Henry arranged for a safari to take them into the deep forest. Charles sat near the shoreline, watching the steamboat being loaded with fruits and vegetables. John Handy came down the well-beaten path, stopping for a moment near the large rock on which Charles sat. "Good luck," said the trainer, extending his hand.

But John Handy did not smile.

"Thank you, sir," said Charles.

"When you strike the next village, ask for a man called Tippu. He has a hut there, filled with necklaces. Tell him you want a leopard's tooth. He'll know what you mean. When he gives it to you, you must take it to Sir Henry, and Sir Henry must wear it all the time he's in Africa. Is that clear?"

"Yes, sir. Is this some sort of . . ."

"Many men have left their bones in this land, Charles." John Handy laid his hand gently on Charles's shoulder. "Africa is old, and there are strange powers in her, stranger than you or I could ever dream of. Sir Henry is under the influence of one, and his life is in danger." John Handy gestured toward the jungle, in which bright birds were singing and screeching. "In the next village. Tell Tippu I said hello." The trainer turned and walked down to the steamer, which was soon underway again, taking him upriver.

"We'll be traveling for two days," said Sir Henry, rolling up the map. Their gear was being distributed among the local men who formed the safari. Their leader was named Kalanga, a young man who moved quietly and efficiently, arranging the loads. He and two packbearers carried food supplies, while Doctor Pickett, Charles, and Sir Henry carried the digging gear.

"Kalanga knows the place I'm looking for," said Sir Henry happily, as the little safari started out.

"Where the old bones are found," said Kalanga, taking the lead on the jungle trail.

Their leader was named Kalanga.

"Quite," said Sir Henry. "Where the old bones are found." He turned to Charles. "I'm not the only one after old bones, you know. The Chinese buy them from the safari traders and grind them up for medicine. Dragon's Bones, they call them. That's how I came to hear of this spot, Dragon Bone Lake, where the old bones are found."

Charles's head was swimming. Dragon bones and jungle lakes! He was surely the happiest boy on the great continent that day. The jungle leaves brushed against him, monkeys chattered above him, and the bright sun rode on high, shining down into forest pools that dotted the winding trail. From the tranquil center of one such pool a hippopotamus suddenly rose, right before Charles's eyes. Huge waves rippled out, touching a bed of floating flowers, from which hundreds of butterflies fluttered. They flew around Charles, touching him with their exotic powders, their wings seeming to whisper to him.

The safari plunged through a hallway of gigantic hanging vines, into deeper country. It was all familiar to Charles, just as he'd dreamt it, and yet it was strange, a thousand times stranger than any dream could ever be. They moved through a vast room of giant mahogany trees, through which the sunlight streamed. Charles felt as if he'd always lived in this land, had always roamed here, among the green corridors.

"Well, of course," said Sir Henry. "This is where man was first born. This is a land with which our souls are deeply familiar. I know the feeling. Yes, I know it well."

They had paused before a crashing forest waterfall. The water foamed and churned close by, and Charles walked with Sir Henry to the edge of the glistening cascade. "The old bones we seek, Charles, are the clues to what our ancestors were like. When you touch one of those bones—when you open the ground and see it there before you, as it has lain for a million years—well, you suddenly feel as if you were that ancient man. It is my belief," said Sir Henry, stooping to wash his face in the water, "that we carry the traces of these men within us."

"But how, Sir Henry!"

"You and your father have certain physical characteristics in common. And your grandfather, Charles, I've seen his picture. You resemble him too. If we could see your great-grandfather and your great-great-grandfather, we'd find other similarities. You are all these men, Charles. They've passed their life on down to you. In a very real way, my boy, they live in you."

Sir Henry stood up from the stream. "So when you touch one of the ancient bones, the ancient men in you respond. That is the thrill of hunting these bones, Charles, that is what draws me. That moment of awakening, when our ancestors speak to us once again, is more wonderful than anything I've ever known. And I want all men to know that feeling, Charles. I want to show them their past and make it live."

Sir Henry tapped his pith helmet with his cane,

giving it the rakish angle he preferred. "And no bloody witch doctor is going to stop me."

"Is that why you quarreled, sir? Over the old bones?"

A wild monkey swung down on a vine, right in front of them. His eyes sparkled brightly and he was munching on a banana, the skin of which he tossed at Sir Henry.

"Little beggar—the old bones? Yes, that was the reason for the quarrel. But that's all over with now. We're far from his part of the jungle."

Beyond the waterfall, the jungle became a dense and intricately woven curtain of vines and leaves, and the men struggled with this heavy-hanging mass of green, hacking their way through it with long bush knives. Charles was at the head of the safari as it emerged from the thickly tangled curtain onto the slopes of a cultivated valley, where women were tending to the earth with their hoes.

"The village is down there," said Kalanga, pointing beyond the fields to a wooded grove, from which numerous wisps of smoke were rising.

The safari slowly descended the sloping hillside, and entered onto the baked earth street of the village. Charles saw small children peeking from the doorways of the thatched-roof huts. In front of other huts, the tribal elders sat in silence.

Charles turned to Kalanga. "Do you know which hut is Tippu's?"

"*Tippu says this is the necklace for you.*"

"That one," said Kalanga, pointing to a hut at the end of the settlement, near a small quiet stream. "Do you have business with him?"

"Yes," said Charles. "I want a leopard's tooth."

"Come," said Kalanga. "I'll speak to him for you."

Charles followed the safari leader down the street. Tippu's hut differed from the others in that its palm leaf walls had been woven with various grasses to produce geometric designs. Tippu was seated inside, on a bed made of tree limbs and palm fronds. His face was covered with red powder and beside him on the bed was a necklace, on which hung a long white tooth!

Charles stared at the tooth in fascination. Seeing the look on Charles's face, Tippu smiled, speaking to Kalanga.

The safari leader translated, saying to Charles: "Tippu says this is the necklace for you."

"But how did he know that I wanted it?"

The old magician rose from his bed and picked up a black lacquered bowl, which held a thin transparent liquid. He pointed to it and again spoke to Kalanga.

"He saw you in his bowl," said Kalanga. "The necklace is made of elephant hairs and a leopard's tooth. It is an Imbamba—a charm to protect you."

The safari set up its lunch table in the middle of the village. The village Chief was seated beside Sir Henry; the Chief's son was beside Doctor Pickett. Charles and Kalanga joined the table in time for a rich feast of wild potatoes and onions, served with broad flat jungle beans.

Sir Henry saw to the teapot, which he tended with great care and from which he poured tea for everyone. Filling the Chief's cup, Sir Henry turned to Kalanga. "Please tell the Chief that in my country tea is the symbol of friendship."

Kalanga translated, and the Chief smiled, raising his cup to Sir Henry. The two men drank, followed by the others, and when the meal was finished, Sir Henry seemed in the best of moods. Quietly then, Charles held out the leopard's-tooth necklace to the scientist. "Sir Henry . . ."

"Yes, Charles?"

"John Handy said that you should wear this while you're in Africa."

Charles expected him to laugh, to make a joke of the necklace, but Sir Henry only said, "This is the tooth of a large cat."

"A leopard's tooth," said Charles.

"Well . . ." Sir Henry quickly looped the necklace around his massive head and settled the tooth inside his shirt. "Perhaps it will bring me good luck on the dig!"

3

Their big square tents were pitched on a high jungle plateau. The sun was setting over a distant lake, the waters of which were turning steadily redder as the great sun-ball sank into them. "That is our destination," said Sir Henry, pointing to the lake. "We should be there by tomorrow noon, according to Kalanga."

The precipice formed a natural barrier against the night-prowling animals. Charles and his father had one tent, Sir Henry another, and Kalanga and the bearers shared a third one. A campfire glowed near the tents. Kalanga sat with the bearers near the edge of the fire, singing soft songs of the jungle. They repeated them slowly over and over, until Charles could no longer distinguish the songs of the men from the songs of the night-birds. He lay in his tent, upon a canvas bunk. A lamp hung from the center of the tent, and Doctor Pickett was reaching up to shut it off.

"I think you'll sleep well tonight."

"Yes, Father," said Charles. "I know I will." His body was tired from the day's march, and the soft songs carried him quickly toward his dreams.

"Everyone have a good night?" Sir Henry was dishing out porridge to the safari. He'd been up long before dawn and had busied himself troubling the cook, tasting the porridge, and burning the toast.

"I dreamt I was playing baseball," said Charles, "back on Riverside Drive."

Sir Henry passed around a bowl of crimson berries. "I dreamt—you may find this strange—I dreamt I was a leopard."

Charles looked up and saw Kalanga turn his head quickly toward the top of the high rock wall beside them, as if he'd heard a footstep there.

"What is it, Kalanga?" asked Sir Henry, who'd also seen the quick movement of the safari leader.

But Kalanga only shook his head and excused himself from the camp table, calling his packbearers to prepare for the day's march.

The expedition crept slowly through densely tangled bush, in the direction of the jungle lake. They could see the lake no longer, for they were in the lowland now, among massive trees that blocked out the sunlight. Through this green gloom they marched, stung by

Through *this green gloom they marched.*

insects and serenaded by fantastically beautiful parrots and birds of paradise. Monstrous spiders walked along over the most delicate flowers, and hundreds of small green snakes hung in the trees. On the soft forest floor Charles found a footprint of a large cat.

"Leopard," said Kalanga, kneeling before the print, which had begun to fill with water.

"The ground is very wet now," said Sir Henry. "We must be close to the lake."

Charles matched his footsteps with Sir Henry's as they continued forward once more. "Excuse me, sir, are you wearing the leopard's tooth?"

"Yes, lad," said Sir Henry, keeping his eyes fixed straight ahead. He reached his hand to his collar and fished out the necklace. The sharp tooth of the leopard swung against his shirt, and a moment later a tiny beam of sunlight struck it, causing the long tooth to glisten like a milky jewel.

"Open ground ahead," said Doctor Pickett, calling back to Charles and Sir Henry. They hurried forward to join the doctor and stepped out of the forest into marshy swampland. Beyond the marsh, Charles saw long-legged flamingos standing in the shining waters of the jungle lake.

"We must circle this way," said Kalanga, pointing toward the right, and they pushed forward through tall cattails and other reeds on which millions of marsh insects crawled.

"What's that!" cried Charles, pointing toward the lake, where a large object was moving toward them through the water, cutting a huge V-shaped wave.

"Crocodile," said Kalanga. "He can't reach us here."

The crocodile was joined by others, and all of them swam along at the edge of the reeds. Charles could hear the snapping of their jaws and the clicking of their teeth. The gnarled heads of the crocodiles followed them around the lake, more and more of the monsters coming along until the shoreline was writhing with scaly tails and bodies. A sudden and terrible bellowing made all of the men turn toward the waters where a gigantic crocodile had risen above the others.

"He is the bull," said Kalanga. "The king of these waters."

The bellowing continued to be heard for at least an hour more as Kalanga led the expedition alongside one of the little streams that fed the lake. "It is mating season," said Kalanga. "The bull is calling to his wives."

The ground all around was porous and spongy, covered with deep green muck. However, Sir Henry's step was more buoyant than ever. "We're standing on the site of an ancient people, Charles. They came to this lake, they drank this water, and they were different, my boy, so different from us!"

Charles had seen the sketches Sir Henry had made of strange men with hairy bodies and apelike faces. Their bones lay hidden here, and he would find one, he knew he would!

4

They made camp in a meadow above the lake. The ground was firm and there was a cool breeze playing with the tent flaps. Everyone was taking his afternoon nap, recovering from the intense jungle heat. But Charles was only half asleep, for he wanted to start digging immediately. He tossed anxiously on his bunk, half-dreaming, seeing the faces of ancient men.

A loud roar brought him instantly awake. For a moment he thought the great bull crocodile must have crawled right into their camp! Doctor Pickett rushed from the tent and Charles followed. Kalanga was at the door of Sir Henry's tent, and Sir Henry came through the flaps, white as a ghost, with beads of perspiration on his brow.

"I'm sorry," he said weakly. "A . . . dream. It was

"A... dream. It was just a dream."

just a dream. The leopard—I dreamt I was a leopard again. Confoundedly real. I woke up roaring."

Kalanga spoke softly. "Did you ever kill a leopard, Sir Henry?"

"I've never killed any sort of animal; don't believe in it. Why do you ask?"

"I thought that perhaps one was haunting you."

"Something I ate has given me a nightmare, that is all. But how vivid it was. I could actually feel my fingers turning into claws."

Strong tea was brought to the camp table, and Doctor Pickett gave Sir Henry a fever tablet. "Not a fever," said Sir Henry, swallowing the tablet, nonetheless. "I feel fine, really. Just a dream, eh? Nothing more . . ."

And quite soon he was his old self again. The possibility for further rest was out of the question, however, all agreed on that, and Sir Henry's suggestion that they begin the dig at once met with quick approval.

The camp boxes were opened and the tools distributed. Kalanga led the way again, but sometimes he stopped completely and closed his eyes, as if receiving a secret signal from the wind. In such moments Charles also tried to remain perfectly still, closing his own eyes and trying to hear the echo of men who had lived long lost ages ago.

But the jungle plain was silent. The expedition moved forward, then separated, each one going on his own, each of the explorers suddenly feeling the urge to search out the missing something they knew lay about here somewhere. Was it a bone? Or an old axhead? Or a broken piece of flint? Surely there is something, thought Charles, for he could feel it in his heart.

He looked around him in the meadow where yellow flowers danced on the ends of long green stems. He walked slowly through them, gold pollen rubbing off on his hands. Closing his eyes, he listened once more. A breeze blew over him lightly, and he let it sway him, as if he were light as a flower on a thin stem. He seemed to hear voices, but very far away, beyond the north horizon somewhere. He turned to the north and started walking. The wind rustled over the flowers, and silky petals touched him on the arms again. He quickened his pace. Something was calling him now, tugging him forward. He started to run through the flowers.

Suddenly Kalanga appeared, rising up out of the high grass, directly in front of Charles. "No," he said, blocking the way.

"But I'm on the dig!" cried Charles. "I can feel it calling me!"

"Many things may call you out here," said Kalanga. "You were running toward your death." He turned and pointed. Moving up the grassy knoll just ahead was a leopard! The cat looked at them, fire blazing in his half-lidded eyes.

Kalanga thrust out his arms and gave a bloodcurdling growl. The cat turned and leapt away out of sight, into the bush.

5

In every direction there were open pits where the digging had gone on. Each day the men took their pickaxes and shovels and added to the network of holes. Now Charles was beside Kalanga on a hillside of sand and stone where they had been digging all morning. Charles was thinking about eating, hoping to hear the dinner gong ring, when suddenly his shovel pierced the hillside, into an empty space. A few more excited strokes and the mouth of a cave opened up. Charles crawled in, taking his lamp with him. Deep inside the cave, the light fell upon a dusty white object.

". . . a man of remotest antiquity," said Sir Henry. The skull was on the camp table. "Observe the large supraorbital ridges . . ."

Doctor Pickett and Kalanga came across the open field, bearing a tray of other bones—ribs, thighbone, toes.

"A brutish man," said Sir Henry joyfully. "Large and powerful . . ."

"Are we ever going to eat again?" Doctor Pickett wiped his brow. The excitement of the find had eclipsed all thought of food, but now each of the men acknowledged the growling in his stomach. The campfire was lit and the meal prepared—again the delicious wild potatoes and onions, served with manioc leaves, which Sir Henry called jungle spinach.

"Bless me," said the scientist, patting his belly as they finished the last of the huge buffet, "I've got to lie down."

"Yes," said Doctor Pickett, "we could all use a little rest. Sunstroke is too easily come by out here."

Doctor Pickett and Sir Henry retired to their bunks. Charles stayed where he was, lounging in the shade of an old acacia tree, as were Kalanga and the pack-bearers. The cool afternoon breeze moved about, whispering through the branches and playing with the butterflies that roamed the field. Charles felt himself slipping off to sleep when a light touch on his arm brought him awake. Kalanga was pointing across the field to the hillside where the cave had been found. Seated in the mouth of the cave was the leopard!

A sudden roar broke the air—a terrible, inhuman cry from Sir Henry's tent. A moment later the flaps burst apart, torn to pieces by Sir Henry leaping forth on his hands and knees. He lifted his head and roared again, the horrible cry wrenching the muscles of his neck and face. His whole body was tensed, and he moved his outstretched hands slowly, as if they'd turned into claws.

"Sir Henry!" Charles cried, as the stricken scientist turned toward him, with a face hideously contorted, the eyes feverishly bright.

Doctor Pickett came from his own tent, hurriedly stepping into his boots. Sir Henry ran off, but Doctor Pickett tackled him to the ground. The two men rolled over in the dust, and Kalanga leapt into the battle, calling to Charles, "The tooth!"

Charles ran to the scientist's tent and seized the necklace from the tentpole where it hung. A second later he stood over the three wrestling men and quickly slipped the tooth-necklace around Sir Henry's neck. Instantly the scientist's muscles relaxed.

"I say, what's going on here?" Sir Henry looked up at Doctor Pickett and Kalanga, and a smile slowly crossed his lips. "Have I been sleepwalking again?"

With trembling hands, Doctor Pickett helped Sir Henry up. "I'm afraid, Sir Henry, it was more serious than that."

"There," said Kalanga softly, and they all turned toward the mouth of the cave, where the leopard still sat, watching.

"You!" cried Sir Henry, waving his fist at the leopard. "How did you find me here!"

The leopard sprang away, disappearing into the high grass. "Imagine the arrogance of that fellow," said Sir Henry, his face livid with rage.

"*How did you find me here!*"

"What fellow?" asked Charles.

"Why, you saw him, sitting there in the mouth of the cave. It was the Tambo witch doctor."

6

I know little of such things," said Kalanga over the evening campfire. The others sat around him, listening to his quiet voice, amidst a chorus of waking nightbirds. "But there are magicians here"—he gestured toward the dark jungle wall—"who can take the shape of certain animals."

As if answering Kalanga, as if he were close by and listening, the leopard roared. Charles felt his stomach tumble and jump as icy fingers walked up his spine.

"It is said that such magicians can turn others into animals, as well." Kalanga glanced toward Sir Henry and then looked back at the glowing fire.

"Bosh!" said Sir Henry. "Pure bosh!"

"Magic, Sir Henry . . ." Doctor Pickett toyed with a twig, touching it to the fire.

". . . is the superstition of the jungle," said Sir Henry sharply. "I'm not going to fall for a lot of hocus-pocus at my age."

"You're in danger," said Kalanga, his voice still soft.

"Danger? Of course," said Sir Henry. "There are a million and one things in this land to kill a man. I'm well aware of that."

Again the leopard roared, closer now, somewhere very close by.

Sir Henry pointed toward the twisted forest shadows. "A hungry leopard is something to worry about. But as for this witch doctor—I've never yet met the man I was afraid of." Sir Henry picked up his crooked walking stick and rapped it on a stone, hard, as if it were his adversary's head.

"Just what sort of quarrel did you have with the witch doctor, Sir Henry?" Doctor Pickett tossed his twig into the fire, where it caught quickly and sparkled up brightly.

"I made fun of his mumbo jumbo. Rude of me, I suppose. But imagine the fellow forbidding me to take any old bones back to England." Sir Henry paused, muttering toward the gnarled head of his stick. "Said the bones belonged to his tribe. I suggested he go rattle his beads at a monkey."

"It is unwise to insult a magician," said one of the packbearers, shaking his head slowly.

"I daresay," replied Sir Henry. "But I have and, what is more, I shall do so again if I catch the fellow prowling around this camp. I shall do more than insult him." Sir Henry bent his stick across his knee, testing its spring. "But what puzzles me is how this so-called witch doctor could have followed us here. His village is hundreds of miles away."

"A magician can walk over the treetops," said the bearer. "He can go from one end of the Great River to the other in the blink of an eye."

"Oh, rot!" said Sir Henry, thumping his stick on the ground.

"I wonder . . ." said Doctor Pickett. "Are we justified in removing these bones from their ancient burial place?"

"Don't be an idiot," said Sir Henry.

"This magician may feel that he's doing his duty, Sir Henry, in protecting the sacred relics of his people."

"No," said Kalanga. "That is not the reason. He wants the old bones because he can make powerful magic with them."

"Kalanga is talking sense," said Sir Henry. "The bones *are* powerful. They are the lost pages of humanity's history. What this witch doctor wants them for is his own business, but he'll have to dig elsewhere. These that we've found"—Sir Henry pointed to the camp table, where the ancient skull was resting—"belong to us."

Doctor Pickett looked across the campfire toward Kalanga, "Do you think we're wrong in taking the bones?"

"You've traveled across the great ocean to find them. I don't believe you will desecrate them."

"Precisely," said Sir Henry. "I wish to elevate these bones to the highest platform and let all people feel their power. Imagine them, Doctor, set in a glass case, illuminated by a gentle spotlight, in some quiet corner of the British Museum—the old bones wouldn't be unhappy." Sir Henry thumped his stick upon the ground again. "Now let's all get a good night's rest. We've got plenty of digging to do in the morning."

"Then I implore you, Sir Henry—" Doctor Pickett pointed to the leopard's tooth, which hung around Sir Henry's neck. "Wear that tooth at all times."

"This thing?" Sir Henry toyed with the tooth. "Well, I shall try to remember. But it's just a tooth, no matter what you say."

"It, too, has power in it," said Kalanga. "Just like the old bones you seek."

"All I know is that it sticks me in the throat when I roll over to sleep."

Charles lay in his bunk, staring at the canvas above his head. Insects continually struck it, their shadows fluttering for a moment and then flying off. "Father," he whispered softly, "Kalanga said that a magician is most powerful when other people are sleeping, that he gets control of them while they're dreaming."

"Unfortunately," said Doctor Pickett with a sigh, "men must sleep."

As if to prove that fact, it was not long before the doctor's heavy breathing showed that he had indeed fallen asleep, and Charles could feel the deep draught

Two malevolent eyes.

of dreams taking him over too. He resisted, but swirling, half-hidden shapes lured him on, down and down, until sleep conquered him completely. He felt light and free, running happily with other animals, when suddenly the herd swerved sharply, and before him he saw the fierce deadly form of the leopard, opening his jaws.

Charles was awake in an instant, for the roar of the leopard was real! Through the mosquito netting he saw two malevolent eyes, gleaming in the darkness.

Doctor Pickett was up with Charles, clutching his rifle. They bolted through the tent door into the clearing. Beyond them, in the brush, a huge beast was running away, breaking branches and snapping small trees.

Charles ran to Sir Henry's tent.

It was empty.

"He's gone," said Charles to his father, who came in behind him. Then Charles saw, hanging by Sir Henry's washstand, the leopard's tooth.

"Bー ut surely Sir Henry must have left a track
somewhere!" said Doctor Pickett. They were
searching all around the camp, shining their lamps on
the ground.

"There is the only track you will find," said Kalanga,
pointing to the four-toed print of a large cat.

Doctor Pickett knelt to examine the clawprint,
shining his light into the dark pointed tips of it, where
the nails had pierced deeply into the earth. "What
animal made it?" asked the doctor.

"A leopard," said Kalanga.

"I was afraid you'd say that."

They followed the leopard's path through the first
tangle of brush, but in the pitch-black shadow of the

jungle night it was impossible to track it further. Returning to the campsite, they sat in front of the fire, where Doctor Pickett cursed himself for not having stood regular watch over Sir Henry.

"It would not have mattered," said Kalanga. "The magician would have lured you away too. He has many spirits helping him."

"Spirits?" Charles looked into Kalanga's eyes, where the dancing firelight was reflected in tiny points of flame.

"They are hidden everywhere in the leaves and in the pools of water. They do his bidding."

"Kalanga, exactly what happened here tonight?" Doctor Pickett withdrew a burning stick from the fire, stared at it for a moment, and tossed it back into the flames.

"Sir Henry became a leopard."

Beside Kalanga, the two packbearers rocked slowly, moaning very softly to themselves. They had been fond of Sir Henry, of his joking way, his generous nature. And by their rocking they seemed to give assent to what Kalanga had just said. But Doctor Pickett was not yet convinced.

"God forbid," said the doctor. "Couldn't it be that a leopard entered the camp and seized Sir Henry bodily and carried him off? That way there would be only the leopard's pawprints, such as we have found."

"A leopard will attack a goat, yes, or an antelope. But he is generally afraid of men. A young boy"—Kalanga turned toward Charles—"he might attempt to

"*Sir Henry became a leopard.*"

carry off a young boy, but it would be impossible for him to carry a man as large as Sir Henry."

"Lycanthropy," said Doctor Pickett, his voice almost a whisper, like the hissing of the flames.

"What did you say, Father?"

"Charles, I fear that Sir Henry has fallen victim to something so strange . . ." The doctor's voice broke off, and he stared wildly into the fire. He seemed lost in thought, then finally lifted his head, glancing toward Charles. "It's from the Greek, *lykos*, meaning wolf. *Anthropos*, meaning man . . ."

"A wolfman!"

"Or in this case, a leopardman. I hesitate to subscribe to such an idea"—Doctor Pickett looked into the fire again—"but what else are we to believe? Lycanthropy—the malady of men who turn into beasts."

8

The exploration party moved through the woods, following the leopard's track. Kalanga and Charles were in the lead, with Doctor Pickett behind them and the packbearers bringing up the rear. The legs of all the men were wet with morning dew, and their boots were already soaked through. They went slowly, for the trail was hard to find. By noontime, they'd traveled no more than a mile. They crouched, they crawled, they struggled on their stomachs and on their backs through a network of vines far from any regular trail. The fleeing leopard had chosen the densest bush for his escape.

At two o'clock they stopped for lunch, quickly erecting a makeshift campsite, for they'd left most of their regular camp gear behind them. Charles took the canvas waterbag and pushed through the brush, toward the murmuring sound of water.

The stream was slow, but of a fair size, and moved lazily along in the shade of overhanging trees. At the water's edge he squatted, lowering the bag into the current. Tiny fish swam near the shoreline, where they were safe from the attacks of larger fish who couldn't navigate in such shallow water. Charles had to watch the mouth of the waterbag, or a little fish would find himself inside it.

Absorbed in watching the fish, he didn't fully perceive a soft rustling sound in the high grass. By the time he realized that something was near—dangerously near—the thing was already there!

He was struck hard from behind, his knees buckled, and he toppled forward into the water. Snapping his head to the side, he found himself staring into cold relentless eyes, which instantly became a blur as a long black shape struck him again. He scrambled in the stream, trying to run, but was held round the ankle by the tail of a twenty-foot python!

He pulled out his knife and struck at the monster, placing a superficial wound in the python's flesh, but deep enough to cause the snake to relax his coiled tail for a moment.

Charles dove for the opposite shore, but the python was after him and lunged onto the bank. Desperately Charles crawled on all fours; the monstrous body crossed over his back and knocked him flat in the mud.

A leopard had leapt upon the python's neck.

Charles flopped like a fish out of water, but the weight of the python was fully upon him; in a moment the great coils would tighten and squeeze the life right out of him.

Then he saw a streak of gold and thought the sun had tumbled out of the sky past his head. He jumped up and found himself witness to a fight more terrible than his own—a leopard had leapt upon the python's neck and was trying to crush the snake in its claws!

The python snapped and shuddered, its black body like the whip of a giant. The leopard held on, spitting ferociously, trying to sink its fangs into the neck of the snake. But the python's tremendous weight and powerful undulations were too much for the cat. He was thrown off, and the snake dove for the water, slithering downstream and out of sight.

The leopard spun around, facing Charles, who was too petrified to move. He'd escaped one monster, only to be threatened by another. His throat was so tight he could hardly breathe, and his knees were trembling violently. But the knife was still in his hand and he was determined to make a good fight of it.

The leopard blinked its eyes sleepily and emitted a loud, rumbling purr. For a second Charles thought he was staring at a large playful house cat—until the beast made its move. With a single leap it was gone into the trees.

9

The expedition party stood with Charles at the site of the battle—the grass was bent and the riverbank covered with pawprints.

"Your knife," said Kalanga. "May I see it?"

Charles still held it in his hand, had been clutching it with all his might ever since the python struck. Now he passed it to Kalanga, who studied its point carefully.

He turned it this way and that, then held it up so that the point glittered in the sunlight. Doctor Pickett stepped alongside him. "What do you see, Kalanga?"

"The snake lost a few scales." Kalanga pointed to the bright bits of black that clung to the cutting edge of the knife.

Charles leaned closer, carefully examining the shining scales. They seemed to be pulsating, like black and sinister stars.

"You should keep these little jewels," said Kalanga, handing the knife back to Charles. He ran his finger up the blade, removing the three glistening bits of snakeskin, which clung lightly to his fingertip.

The treetops suddenly rustled, as a wind from nowhere came upon them. The sky opened and raindrops large as silver dollars came crashing down. It was a jungle storm, as sudden and ferocious as any wild beast, shredding the leaves and dashing them to the forest floor.

The expedition party took cover beneath a large old umbrella tree, but it did little good, for the tree was moaning and sighing, and the rain passed right through its foliage. Vaporous mist moved in among the tree roots and along the bank of the stream, where a thousand tiny rivulets had suddenly formed.

Then, as quickly as it had come, the storm ended. The sun once again sparkled on the leaves, and the parrots, sunbirds and weavers resumed their cries. But the men were soaking wet, their clothes and bodies streaming with water. Charles looked at his fingertip. The scales of the python were gone, washed away in the downpour.

Kalanga nodded his head. "The magician has the jungle spirits to help him. They took his jewels from you."

Charles looked at Kalanga, and at the packbearers, who were also nodding their heads, as if the whole

The expedition party took cover.

affair was perfectly clear to them. "I don't understand," said Charles.

"It was a magic python," said Kalanga. "Never have I seen such scales before, like diamonds. And I've known many pythons."

"Yes, yes," said one of the packbearers. "What Kalanga says is true. We had a python in our village, a pet. Very strange too. He sometimes went a whole year without eating a bite of food. But he wasn't magic, just a little crazy."

"Or particular," said the other packbearer.

"But he was real. And this python who left the jewels behind him today—he wasn't real. He was magically produced."

"By the Tambo magician?" asked Doctor Pickett.

"I believe so," said Kalanga.

"And the leopard?"

"It was Sir Henry!" cried Charles.

"You speak the truth," said Kalanga. "The leopard was Sir Henry. The tracks I saw here, before the storm washed them away, were the same tracks we've been following since Sir Henry disappeared."

"But why didn't he stay close by us?" asked Doctor Pickett.

"His heart is a leopard," said Kalanga. "His head is a leopard. His tail is a leopard. Only a tiny part of him is still a man, and it's so small he cannot really understand what it says. It spoke to him, though, and forced him to save your son's life. It is like a single tooth in the leopard's mouth, one tooth that remembers."

"Well, then, we've got to find that leopard," said Doctor Pickett. "And remind him who he really is."

"The trail," said Charles, pointing into the treetops, "is that way."

"Do you have the leopard's tooth?" asked Kalanga.

"Yes," said Charles, "it's in my pack."

"You must wear it now, for the magician may attack you again."

Charles went to his pack and withdrew the leopard's tooth. Slowly he slipped it around his neck. As the tooth touched his bare flesh, he felt a thrill run along his spine, and the hairs on the back of his neck bristled up, like a hissing cat's.

10

The trail of the leopard was impossible to follow; the jungle treetops left no trace of the swiftly moving cat, except for terrified monkeys. And their chattering network spread so rapidly and in so many directions that the search party stood baffled in the midst of a howling symphony.

A beautiful sunbird came along, crying loudly and flying very low over them.

"That is our omen," said Kalanga. "We must go in that direction."

They pushed on, hoping to pick up the trail, and entered a wilderness of thick, scummy quagmire, nauseating to breathe. The mucky bottom of the swamp made horrible sucking noises with each footstep they took, like mouths that wanted to swallow them down. Bugs of every sort attacked them, biting the soft flesh of their eyelids, swelling them and obscuring their vision.

Through the heavy green curtain of the swamp trees the sun worked its way, casting a soft gentle light on grotesque toadstools and other fleshy fungus growths. Clinging to the roots and branches of the trees were beautiful little toads, their bright colors chimerical and lovely. Overhead were enormous orchids, ten feet high, like flowers in a dream.

"Don't scratch your bites, Charles," said Doctor Pickett. "You'll only make them worse."

But they were all scratching, bitten by ticks, fleas, mosquitoes. Razor grass and swamp thistle tore at their clothes and their bare flesh. They collapsed in the duckweed and rose, gasping and sputtering, pushing their way forward, hoping for solid ground again and finding only more of the endless green gloom.

Then the sunbird appeared once more, high up on a branch, and the search party plunged on, trusting in the omen. They lashed at the weeds that obstructed them; but the roots were tough and caught them up again and again, hobbling and tripping them.

On the surface of the water were huge insects, long-legged water-boatmen, paddling along in the waves made by the stumbling search party. A large, lazy golden fish came swimming by, its mouth working slowly, its movement stagnant as the swamp itself. Charles felt as if he were in the garden of a mad giant, who might at any moment appear through the weeds and carry them off.

"We cannot go on," said Kalanga, as the search party gathered round a gigantic rotting tree stump.

"Yes," said one of the bearers. "Our death will surely find us here."

"Agreed," said Doctor Pickett, whose face was streaked with the blood of a thousand bugbites.

"But what of Sir Henry?" Charles asked.

"Our only hope," said Kalanga, "is that Sir Henry will return to the place of his beloved bones."

"You mean the dig?" asked Doctor Pickett.

"It was a powerful place for him," said the other bearer. "Now he may seek it out again."

Doctor Pickett took out his compass and brought it close to his swollen eyelids. Unable to see clearly, he handed it to Charles.

Charles held the black metal case in his palm and waited for the needle to come to rest. "That way," he said, pointing with his finger toward a distant tree, out of which the sunbird suddenly flew, crying wildly.

"Little deceiver!" cried a packbearer.

"Yes," said Kalanga softly. "He certainly tricked us, didn't he."

The dig was still intact—the hillside open, the piles of dirt untouched—but the jungle creepers had already begun winding themselves around the camp chairs and table, giving the campsite a look of bewitchment. The bearers quickly cut back the creepers and the tent

"*That way.*"

ropes were drawn tight again. Nonetheless, the atmosphere continued to be oppressive, and Charles felt that he was being watched by some unseen power. Kalanga said it was a *moena*—an evil spirit in the employ of the magician.

The ancient skull on the camp table did not help matters any. Its hollow eyes seemed to follow one's every move, and its crooked mouth smiled night and day, as if enjoying some sly, eternal joke. "Would anyone mind terribly if I covered this thing?" asked Doctor Pickett, midway through their first week of waiting.

No one minded. The doctor placed a water bucket around the skull.

The shovels and digging picks remained unused. It seemed bad luck to continue with the very thing that had brought about Sir Henry's misfortune. So the days passed slowly, in idleness. The nights were lonely, with each man taking a turn at the campfire, feeding it and standing guard. Charles saw many things in the flames—strange figures, which leapt forth and disappeared in the jungle wall. He didn't know if he'd dreamt them or really seen them, but every night it was the same—the campfire and the trees seemed haunted.

"They are the *lume-lume*," said one of the bearers. "The shades of night."

"Are they dangerous?"

"Not to you. You wear the magic talisman," said the bearer, pointing to the leopard's-tooth necklace.

But the necklace brought Charles no comfort when he was squatting alone by the fire. He closed his eyes but the *lume-lume* seemed to pass right through his eyelids. They were ugly, fearful beings, resembling men, but not completely. They had the fangs of a cat, and they laughed hideously, gnashing their teeth at him. Often he longed to cry out, to call for his father, but he held on somehow, refusing to give in. And when the sudden sunrise came, turning the jungle into a gloriously warm and beautiful jewel-room, he was glad that he'd kept his nerve.

"The quinine is nearly gone," said Doctor Pickett, midway through their third week of waiting.

They knew now they could stay no longer. Though food was available—there were wild beans and pumpkins and a fruit the doctor identified as the phrynia berry—quinine was their only protection against the worst jungle enemy, malarial fever.

The tents came down and were rolled up, the camp chairs were folded, the cook pots were strung on the rucksacks. All that remained of the old campsite were the bones, which now occupied the center of the clearing on the ground.

"I believe we should put these back where we found them." Doctor Pickett looked around at the other members of the expedition.

"Yes," said Kalanga. "They have brought us no luck."

The bones were carried up the hillside to the mouth of the cave from which they'd come. Charles lit the lantern and crawled back to the deepest recess of the cave. The bones were passed in to him and he arranged them carefully, not really knowing why. It seemed irreverent to just toss down these age-old relics. He knew now what Sir Henry had meant—he suddenly felt as if this cave were his home; he was an ancient man, filled with an intense awareness of exactly how it was to live long ago. And then time closed again and he was merely Charles Pickett, a boy of thirteen.

Outside he heard Kalanga and the packbearers chanting in Swahili, and he knew that they too were feeling something rooted deep in themselves. They too could feel the power of the ancient being who dwelled in their hearts. As he crawled from the cave, they were dancing slowly around the hillside and he joined them, while Doctor Pickett recited a prayer for the man who'd lived when the earth was young, 500,000 years ago. Somehow Doctor Pickett hoped the prayer would reach Sir Henry, too—wherever he was.

11

"C an we see Tippu again?" Charles asked.

They stood in the middle of the little jungle village once more. Tame monkeys screeched at them from the rooftops and the old village men sat as before, watching with stonelike calm everything that came and went.

Kalanga led the expedition party to Tippu's hut. The sorcerer greeted them with a green banana snake visiting on his neck. Doctor Pickett and Charles stood in silence as Kalanga explained to the old sorcerer what had happened. The banana snake crawled up and put his nose in the sorcerer's ear, tickling him, then traveled down the sorcerer's arm, disappearing under the large bed.

Charles stared at the ceiling where a variety of dried plants were hanging, along with the bright shells and beads and lacquered bowls with strange markings on them. "Will he be able to see Sir Henry in his bowl?"

"No," said Kalanga. "He says that he must perform a magic dance in order to see something so obscure as a man hidden within a leopard."

Tippu led them along a well-beaten path to a cleared spot behind his hut. The green banana snake followed, slithering through the leaves. The old man quickly drew a circle in the sand; Charles saw that the design he made within it was similar to the geometric pattern that was woven into the walls of his hut.

The sorcerer danced, beating a small drum, and whirled, ringing a little bell. He was forced to chase the banana snake out of the magic circle, explaining that the snake might be injured by the powerful forces he was appealing to. The snake crawled onto Charles's shoe and lay there like a long, living shoelace.

Once again the sorcerer danced and whirled, concluding his ritual by the tossing of a pair of dice, on which abstract figures had been traced. He knelt, studying them, and turned to Kalanga with an explanation. Kalanga listened and pointed to Charles. "The Power says that you must put the leopard-tooth necklace around Sir Henry's neck. You will meet again in a cave beneath the surface of the great ocean."

"But how?" cried Charles. "How can I get into an ocean cave?" His mind was suddenly filled with thoughts of diving bells and deep-sea suits and giant

Once again the sorcerer danced.

octopi hiding in great underwater caverns.

"I'm afraid, Charles," said Doctor Pickett gently, "that we have done all we can. The trail has been lost." He knew that Charles was starting to suffer from fever; his own brain was all a-jumble. He was concerned for their health and he couldn't deal with any more of this magical business. "Thank Tippu for us, Kalanga. We appreciate his efforts. I should like to continue our march now. There's a good bit of daylight left."

They pushed on through the forest, down hallways of tall teak and ebony trees, whose branches were wound with flowering lianas. But Charles knew now that behind this lovely network there lurked strange forces, visible and invisible. He vowed that he would return to Africa to learn more; and with a shudder he realized that he, like Sir Henry, had fallen under the magician's spell. He seemed to hear Sir Henry's voice now, somewhere amidst the cries of the lemurs and parrots:

". . . *return to Africa again and again.*"

"I'll help you, Sir Henry, don't worry."

"What did you say, Charles?" his father asked.

"I was talking to Sir Henry."

Doctor Pickett shook his head and urged the safari on more quickly. The boy was definitely suffering fever-dreams and the sooner they got back to civilization the better.

But Charles didn't feel feverish, though it may have appeared that way on the surface. He felt radiantly strong, with his ears attuned to the hidden jungle voices. The fearful *lume-lume*, the shadows of the night, had initiated him into the inner world of the forest. The parasol trees, if he just squinted his eyes a little, turned into beautiful beings, fantastic and wonderfully alive, adorned with many arms and bright jewels. There were two jungles—one which everyone saw, and another one, which would appear if he let it, if he didn't run scared from it. It was in the dancing fire and in the gently spreading trees. It was the hidden world, a land of rare and delightful creatures, as well as some terrible ones, and Charles had found its doorway. The door was everywhere, in every leaf and twisting root. He knew that this was the doorway that magicians find and pass through, and he asked the parasol beings to help him find Sir Henry. They answered that they would.

"Where?" asked Charles.

"In a cave beneath the ocean."

Finally the jungle gave way, and they came once
again to the village of One Thousand Huts on the
bank of the Congo River. The huts were much like
American cottages, with gently sloping roofs and
plaster walls. Walking through this large busy village,
Charles felt the inner voice of the jungle grow silent.
Here were only the voices of men, busily engaged in
trade. He knew that he'd lost something wonderful,
which could be found only in the heart of the forest,
and he vowed to return to that heart. *"Once you go
deep into its forests, you'll return. . . ."*

Again Sir Henry's voice touched him faintly, but was
quickly lost in the hustle and bustle of the traffic to the
river's edge. Nonetheless, Charles was certain that he

understood the voice, that it was the jungle telling him that he would be a scientist like Sir Henry, that he would study and come back to the enchanted glades and pools where the parasol beings danced in the sunlight. And he would find the ancient bones, the relics that made him feel not like a boy of thirteen, but like a man whose age could not be reckoned, a man of long, long ago. He felt that he was this man deep inside, a man who had never really died, but who'd had his tiny spark passed on and on.

Charles walked to the river on which the sun was blazing like an immense diamond. He felt like the sun, as if his body were made of a million tiny flames, a billion tiny flames, his billion ancestors. This was life, and life was the greatest magic of all.

Each day he went to the pier and stood there, watching upriver for the little steamboat, *Maria*. The great Congo River rolled past slowly, had been rolling for countless ages, and would roll for many more. Staring at it, he became the river, rolling endlessly to the sea, to where Tippu said he would meet Sir Henry again, in a cave beneath the great ocean.

"Steamboat coming!"

The pier was soon crowded with villagers bringing their trade goods, and Charles was at the very end of the pier as the deckhand on the *Maria* tossed his line. The Captain nosed the steamboat against the creaking wooden pilings, and the lines were quickly made fast. The crew began taking on fuel and cargo. Kalanga and the packbearers handed over the luggage and expedi-

"*Good-bye, Kalanga.*"

tion gear to the sailors, and Doctor Pickett purchased tickets for himself and Charles.

"Good-bye, Kalanga." Doctor Pickett extended his hand.

"I am sorry, sir," said Kalanga, taking the doctor's hand in his own. "If I had been a proper guide, Sir Henry would be sailing with you today."

"Don't talk nonsense."

"I'll continue the search," said Kalanga. "I know the print of this leopard as well as my own face." He turned to Charles, started to extend his hand, and brought it back to his side. For a moment he stared into the boy's eyes, seeing there the look of a man-of-the-forest, one who knew about the hidden world. Kalanga curled his fingers into a fist and tapped Charles lightly on the heart.

"Look for me when you come back." Kalanga turned, and was quickly lost among the many men moving along the shoreline.

13

I'm most unhappy to hear of the misfortune that befell Sir Henry," said the Customs Chief in the large seaport at the mouth of the Congo. "He was killed by a leopard, you say?"

"That is what we believe," said Doctor Pickett, who felt it better not to explain the mysterious circumstances under which Sir Henry had left the expedition. He stared down sadly at the tip of Sir Henry's cane, which he carried with him constantly now, as a reminder of the deep friendship he had known with the jovial scientist.

A ship's horn blew in the harbor. Charles felt a sudden burning on his neck, where the leopard's tooth hung.

"The *Lovely Anne*," said the Customs Chief, turning to the window and nodding toward the ship. "She sails in a few minutes for England. You fellows will be sailing tomorrow for America, eh?"

"Father," said Charles, "we've got to be on that ship!" He pointed toward the *Lovely Anne*, whose crew was already preparing to raise the gangplank.

"But Charles, it's going to England, not America."

"Father," said Charles, "we must!" The leopard's tooth was flaming against his skin now, like the tip of a branding iron.

Doctor Pickett looked into Charles's eyes and saw something he'd never seen before— a spark of manhood, of certainty—and it shook him to the core. "Very well," he said, and they raced out of the Customs House and through the streets of the seaport. They had no tickets, and their baggage was already aboard the ship to America, but they were running toward the gangplank of the *Lovely Anne*!

"Stop!" shouted Doctor Pickett. "We must board!"

The deckhand looked puzzled for a moment, but the Ship's Purser ordered the gangplank to be lowered again. The Picketts clattered up it breathlessly.

While Doctor Pickett was completing transactions with the Purser, Charles started wandering the deck of the ship, as disoriented as if he were still in deep, tractless jungle. But the leopard's tooth around his neck was burning, hotter and hotter, and he felt that something on board the ship must be causing it. He circled the deck slowly. As he passed a green door with a porthole in it, the tooth actually gave him a burning bite.

Charles hauled the heavy sea-door open and stepped into a dimly lit passageway that carried him down and around, down and around, down and around into the below-deck of the ship, to the cargo hold. Merchant seamen were working there, arranging numerous boxes and bales. The air was close and damp, yet strangely enough it smelled like the jungle. What was that familiar smell, like that of an elephant!

As if answering his question, the loud trumpeting of an elephant sounded from the next hold. Charles walked toward it and reached for the door, but it swung open in front of him.

"John Handy!"

"Charles, what are you . . ."

At once the animal trainer saw the peculiar look in the boy's eyes, which seemed to be fixed by a burning mystery. It was a look familiar to him—all those who have been touched by the ghostly hands of the jungle wear it. "What are you looking for, Charles?" he asked softly. Charles pointed beyond John Handy to a cage in the second hold where an enormous leopard was pacing about.

Within Charles's head the words of Tippu were echoing, over and over: *You will meet in a cave beneath the surface of the great ocean.*

John Handy stepped aside, letting Charles pass. He walked toward the leopard. All around, on every side, were other caged animals—the chained elephant, as well as monkeys, chimps, and a long black python.

But Charles could see only the leopard, whose bright eyes flashed in the dim-lit hold.

"Be careful, Charles," said John Handy. "The leopard is the most unpredictable of all creatures."

Charles removed the leopard's-tooth necklace from under his shirt. "I must put this around his neck."

John Handy remained silent for a moment. He felt the electricity in the air. This young lad was as intent as a leopard. The mood was right, a special mood John Handy always had whenever he dealt with a wild animal. Charles and the leopard were staring at each other, their bodies swaying together.

John Handy reached for the cage door. The leopard snarled toward the trainer, his vicious teeth glistening.

Charles moved forward, and the leopard became silent again as Charles took hold of the cage door. The leopard sat back and licked its paw.

"All right," said John Handy, "it's your show. Go in slowly and you can master him."

Charles took another step toward the door. John Handy touched his shoulder lightly. "You're not afraid?"

"No," said Charles.

"Good. Don't lose your nerve for a moment. It's your control over him, and every trainer must have such a control. If he senses your fear, he'll spring at you." John Handy stood silently at the door. He could see the boy was ready for a great test. He had to let him try. One simply could not stand in the way of such things.

The trainer opened the door slowly. Charles stepped

into the cage. The leopard sat staring at him for a moment and then went back to washing its paws. Charles moved a step closer. The tooth was smouldering on his neck, radiant as an ember from a jungle fire, but he no longer felt its heat. All of his concentration was on the eyes of the beast before him, a huge jungle-cat whose fangs were dripping saliva.

Beyond the bars, beads of sweat were pouring from John Handy's face. He was responsible for the lad's life, and the chance was a terrible one. There was no more dangerous animal than a leopard. They didn't make good show cats, so unreliable were they, and here was an untrained boy advancing on one. But if he can control this cat, thought John Handy, he'll never fear anything again.

"That's it, Charles," said John Handy softly, "move in on him slowly. It's your will over his."

Charles felt as if his arms were being lifted for him, at the elbows, by gentle invisible hands. His body had suddenly become very light, and his movements were slow and smoothly flowing. The necklace was in his hands and he was bringing it toward the leopard's head.

The leopard stared at the necklace and then suddenly swung its paw. Charles pulled the necklace back, as the claws whizzed past him. He was shaking now; his knees were going to buckle, and the leopard was advancing on him.

"Many a time I said to myself, this is it. We'll never get out of this one. . . ." The voice of the old sailor,

Mr. Wyman, came in his ears, steadying him as the leopard sprang. Charles sidestepped and slipped the necklace swiftly around the big cat's neck.

"Excellent!" cried John Handy. "Well done!" But what in heaven's name . . .

The captive gorilla pounded his chest, the elephant screamed, the chimps cried out. The leopard had gone into a convulsion, shuddering terribly. Charles watched in horrible fascination as the animal's body suddenly lost its solidity. Howling madly, the leopard collapsed into an amorphous lump of quivering energy —a golden ball, spotted with black, like a miniature sun with sunspots upon it.

The dark spotted whorls erupted violently from the golden surface. The hold of the ship was filled with light emanating from the golden shape. It stretched itself, shuddered again, its molecules engaged in some nightmarish dance of power. It seemed like the trembling of the first gas at the beginning of time, like a miniature universe in upheaval, whirling and burning wildly, seeking to shape itself. Tossing upon this cosmic sea of light was the leopard's-tooth necklace, encircling the burning gas and keeping it from dissolving into space.

The colorful mass emitted a low groaning sound. A sunspot burst open, and a roar came from it. The black spot opened wider, white stones appearing and a red carpet . . .

Teeth and tongue!

"Help . . . help me . . ." The mouth cried out to

"Sir Henry!"

the dark hold, and two more sunspots erupted. Blue liquid filled the holes, swirling around, solidifying, gazing outward. They were eyes.

And the strange shuddering mass heaved all at once, its stuff growing more dense and closely packed. A leg, two, the head, the neck, the whole body of . . .

"Sir Henry!"

His eyes were dazed and he stared around him like a man waking from a deep and troubled dream. But before Charles or John Handy could make a move toward Sir Henry, a loud hiss made them turn their heads.

"How the devil did he get free!" John Handy leapt toward the black python. The snake coiled itself around the trainer's struggling leg. Sir Henry joined the fight, grabbing the huge snake by the throat, and Charles tackled it in the middle.

The monster thrashed and squirmed, its tremendous muscles flexing like bands of springing steel. The men rolled with him, as the great python tried to coil itself around all three of them, crashing from one cage to another, banging against the bars.

It was into this infernal cave of shouts and curses that Doctor Pickett stepped, still carrying Sir Henry's cane. Seeing the wild struggle, he raced forward, swung the cane with all his might, and delivered a shattering blow to the snake's head.

The creature exploded into a thousand tiny scales. The scales glittered like diamonds, forming themselves into the vague shape of a man, a ghostly-walking,

It was the Tambo witch doctor.

glittering man, with eyes no less cold than those of a snake. It was the Tambo witch doctor, and smiling malevolently, he bowed to the group and vanished from their midst.

"Gone!" cried Sir Henry. "If I catch that fellow around this camp again . . ." He paused, looking around the dark hold of the ship. "I say, what has become of our camp?"

14

Sir Henry could remember nothing from the time he said good-night to Doctor Pickett, Charles, and Kalanga a month ago in the jungle, until he'd awakened in the ship's hold. "All right, I'll be an utter fool and agree with you three chaps that I was a leopard. You say it's true, so it must be. So there are real magicians walking around in the jungle, or flying over the treetops for all I know. But I'm not done digging old bones there, not by a long shot!"

"You had better take good care of your leopard's tooth, then," said John Handy.

"Yes, I'll purchase several more of them, too," said Sir Henry. "And sew them into my underwear. But I'll be going back there, I promise you. And if that

"Take good care of your leopard's tooth..."

magician fellow comes around our camp, he'll have my stick to contend with." Sir Henry tapped it on the ship's railing, where the ocean moonlight caught the tip of it, causing it to flash as if encrusted with shining snake's scales.

Doctor Pickett touched the moon-struck tip. "I'd say this was a very lucky walking stick, Sir Henry."

"Been in the family for ages. The ancestral war club, eh?"

"Make no mistake about it," said John Handy. "The good men who held that stick in their own lifetime imparted a real power to it. Shall we say—they left their mark upon it."

"I only hope it left a mark on that witch doctor's head," said Sir Henry. "Although I'm taking a rather different view of the fellow lately."

"What do you mean, Sir Henry?" asked Charles.

"Well, you know, he's after the old bones and so am I. It's not the first time a pair of collectors have clashed over such things. Cuvier and Lamarck nearly came to blows over the bones of a Tertiary opossum. And Professor Cope and Professor Marsh quarreled bitterly over a Triassic dinosaur bone. Hurled rocks at each other and rolled around in the fossil deposits trying to strangle one another. So I look upon this witch doctor as a somewhat excitable fellow seeker. Next time I travel to Africa, I shall send him a 50,000-year-old skull as a gift!"

"Sir Henry," said John Handy, "that might not be a bad idea, at all!"

15

Because of the unexpected trip to England, Charles and Doctor Pickett were able to visit with Sir Henry at Turnbull Manor. There were many old bones there, including an Ornithischian pelvis that rolled out of the cupboard when he opened it to give them tea.

The Picketts would certainly have stayed longer in Sir Henry's strange old country house, but school was soon to resume in New York City. After sending off a telegram to Kalanga's village, telling their guide that all was well, that Sir Henry had been found, they boarded another ship and made a peaceful crossing of the Atlantic, with the adventure already starting to fade in their minds, as if it were a dream. Yet a dream it was not, for the reality of it had been branded upon them. On Charles's neck where the leopard's tooth had hung, there was now a scar in the shape of a tooth, clear and perfectly outlined as a sailor's tattoo.

"Well, Wyman," said Doctor Pickett, as they again entered the house on Riverside Drive.

"You're looking well, sir," said Wyman.

"Has Mrs. Pickett returned yet?"

"Still in Egypt, sir, poking about in the tombs."

"We'll have a thing or two to tell her when she comes home," said Doctor Pickett with a smile.

"Is that so, sir?" said Wyman. "A few of the shipmates are in the back room. Come and join us for some tea and a bit of cheese."

At that moment the door to the back room opened and old Captain Nugent appeared. With him were the two other old sailors, the little one with the eye patch and the big one with the eagle tattooed on his bald head.

"Come on, Doctor," called Captain Nugent. "Give us the full of it. You've been halfway round the world."

In days gone by, Doctor Pickett had listened to these old salts spin their adventures long into the night. Often he'd wanted to join in, but he'd had nothing to tell about. So it was with a gleam in his eye that he pulled up a chair, motioning Charles to sit beside him.

"Show them where the leopard's tooth hung, Charles."

Charles opened his shirt collar, and Captain Nugent peered closely at the strangely shaped scar. "Well, lad, that's quite a thing, isn't it!"

And so the tale of the leopard's tooth began.

NEW FROM BARD
DISTINGUISHED MODERN FICTION

TOAD OF TOAD HALL
A.A. Milne   58115-9/$2.95

This stage version of Kenneth Grahame's classic novel *THE WIND IN THE WILLOWS*, by the author of *WINNIE THE POOH* brings to life the comic, splendid world of the River Bank, and the misadventures of the unforgettable Mr. Toad.

STATUES IN A GARDEN
Isabel Colegate   60368-3/$2.95

A novel of an upperclass Edwardian family and the tragedy that befalls them when a forbidden passion comes to fruition. "Beautifully graduated, skillfully developed...Isabel Colegate is a master."*The New York Times Book Review*

THE MOUSE AND HIS CHILD
Russell Hoban   60459-0/$2.95

"Like the fantasies of Tolkein, Thurber, E.B. White, THE MOUSE AND HIS CHILD is filled with symbolism and satire, violence and vengeance, tears and laughter."*The New York Times*. By the author of the widely acclaimed novel RIDDLEY WALKER.

REDISCOVERY
Betzy Dinesen, Editor   60756-5/$3.50

A remarkable collection of 22 stories by and about women, written over a period of 300 years and structured to explore the life-cycle of a woman. These stories reveal the perceptions of women writers, past and present, showing how these women responded to the restrictions and exploited the opportunities—literary and social—of their age.

Avon Paperbacks